"Love as powerful as your mother's for you leaves its own mark."
- J. K. Rowling

Before we begin, before you read this tale,

You need to know about a lady, who cared a lot about whales,

This lady was Fiona, and of this story - she is the owner,

Because when I was a little girl, with my cherub-like curls,

My Mum created this story, so for that she deserves all the glory.

Each night she would tuck me in, and I would give her a grin,

Because I knew the routine, she was the story-telling Queen.

She would tell me about five little bunnies, and the stories were rather funny,

And these moments before bed, all the stories she read,

Will stay with me forever, and I will endeavour,

To let these memories live on, because although she is gone,

My Mum was the best, those who knew her will attest,

To have her as my Mum, was second to none,

And so when you read this book, I want you to look,

Into the stars, and know she's never that far,

Because her memories live on, and from our hearts - she is never gone.

Once upon a time there were five little bunnies. Their names were Bobby, Belinda, Barbara, Billy and Boris.

The bunnies lived in the countryside, in burrows under the grass. Their best friend lived nearby, a dog named Buster - who was known for running very fast.

One summer's morning, the bunnies and Buster packed a picnic and headed out.
They took with them their new kite, they were excited to run about.

They went to a meadow, filled with pretty flowers. "Look how beautiful these are," shouted Belinda, "I could smell them for hours!"

After a short walk, the friends sat down to talk. They decided that the wind was just right, to play with their kite.

Billy took charge and started running with the kite, he threw it in the air, and it took its' flight.

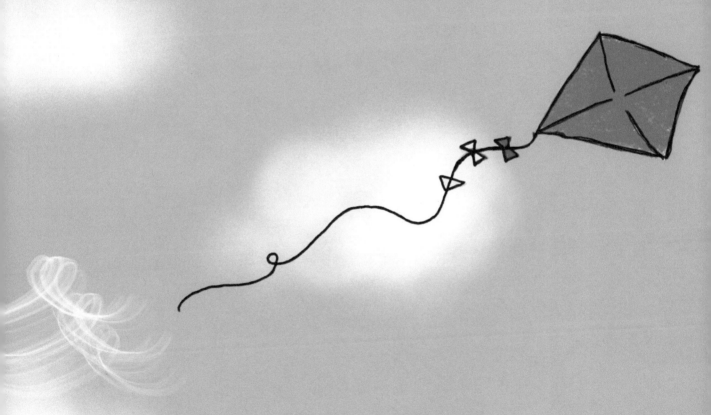

But suddenly came a gust of wind, and Billy let go of the string. "Oh no!" Cried Boris, "it's going to fly away!"
"We can't let that happen", said Billy, "We only got it the other day!"

As quick as a flash, Buster chased after the kite. He ran and he ran, almost the speed of light!

But the bunnies stood still, it all happened so fast. They watched Buster go, their faces aghast.

"What do we do?" Said Barbara. Buster is gone!

Over here! Yelled Bobby, "Jump on! Jump on!"

The bunnies followed Bobby's voice, through some bushes and leaves. And there Bobby was, behind some trees.

Bobby had found a hot air balloon. "We can use this!" He said, "We can rise up high, up into the sky and we can look for Buster". "Hmm," pondered Belinda, "I guess it's worth a try!"

The bunnies hopped on, and they started their ascent. They travelled through the clouds, up and away they went.

"I can't see him, can you?" said Barbara, she was starting to worry. "I see him!" Yelled Boris, "come on! Let's hurry!"

Down below they saw, the kite stuck in a tree. And then they spotted Buster, trying to get it free.

"When we get down, we need to head for that tree. To make sure we don't get lost - remember it's between those sweet peas"
said Billy.

The bunnies got to the ground and ran to the sweet peas. "You found me!" Buster cheered, "Please set me free!"

Buster was all tied up, tangled in the kite. "Oh Buster I'm so glad we found you" said Belinda, "you gave us a fright!"

The bunnies helped Buster, untangling him from the kite. "Well I don't know about you" said Buster, "but I've worked up an appetite!"

They laid out the picnic and sat down to eat, the bunnies and Buster were glad to rest their feet.

"Well," said Barbara, "what an interesting day! I think we should head home now, the clouds are starting to look grey."

Buster thanked the bunnies, for coming to his rescue. "We would always do that" said Boris, "that's because we love you."

The bunnies and Buster made their way home, talking about the next adventure, and where they're going to go.

The End... until the next adventure.

Lightning Source UK Ltd.
Milton Keynes UK
UKHW051542130421
381891UK00001B/36